STAR WARS

THE FORCE AWAKENS

REY'S STORY

WRITTEN BY ELIZABETH SCHAEFER

BASED ON THE SCREENPLAY BY
LAWRENCE KASDAN & J. J. ABRAMS
AND
MICHAEL ARNDT

DISNEY

LUCASFILM
PRESS

LOS ANGELES · NEW YORK

P9-CEX-772

To the next generation of Jedi
—ES

For information address Disney • Lucasfilm Press,
1101 Flower Street, Glendale, California 91201.
Printed in the United States of America
First Edition, February 2016
1 3 5 7 9 10 8 6 4 2
FAC-029261-16015
ISBN 978-1-4847-7409-0
Library of Congress Control Number on file

SUSTAINABLE
FORESTRY
INITIATIVE
Certified Sourcing
www.sfiprogram.org
SFI-01415

Cover and interior art by Brian Rood

Visit the official *Star Wars* website at: www.starwars.com.

CONTENTS

PROLOGUE 1

CHAPTER 1 7

CHAPTER 2 17

CHAPTER 3 25

CHAPTER 4 33

CHAPTER 5 43

CHAPTER 6 51

CHAPTER 7 57

CHAPTER 8 65

CHAPTER 9 73

CHAPTER 10 81

CHAPTER 11 91

CHAPTER 12 97

CHAPTER 13 105

CHAPTER 14 115

CHAPTER 15 123

EPILOGUE 133

PROLOGUE

THE ASTEROID WAS QUIET. The great rocky mountains on its surface cast long shadows over high ridges and deep caves. Any sensors would bounce off the heavy metal ores that ran all the way through the floating rock.

It was the perfect place to hide.

Rey nudged her A-wing fighter forward. The ship lurched as the asteroid's gravity pulled it down, but Rey quickly adjusted her course. This wasn't her first time flying through an asteroid field. If she timed it *just* right, she could disappear into one of the caves below and—

Blaster fire scorched the wing of Rey's ship! It was too late. The TIE fighter had found her.

Rey immediately fired her thrusters to their max and dove into the nearest cave. The enemy ship tried to follow, but it couldn't make the turn in time. The TIE zoomed past the cave entrance before whipping back to track her down.

Stupid, stupid, stupid. Rey mentally kicked herself for letting the enemy sneak up on her like that. Taking a deep breath, Rey refocused and flew farther into the branching cave. She was certain that one of the tunnels *must* lead back to the surface.

She could hear the screech of the engines as the TIE closed in on her. If she didn't come up with a plan soon, she was going to run out of cave. Her sensors bounced uselessly off the rocks around her. But even without their guidance, Rey could see the walls were getting closer and closer. The only way out now was behind her.

Behind me . . . Rey smiled. She had a crazy idea.

If her sensors were malfunctioning, there was a good chance the TIE fighter's were, too. Slowly, Rey eased off her thrusters and took her ship as close to the cave floor as she could. She almost heard the pebbles vibrating beneath her as she skimmed along. One centimeter too low and her A-wing would be a pile of rubble.

Rey heard the TIE's engines grow louder and louder. *Not yet.*

The cave began to rumble as the enemy ship drew closer. *Almost there.*

The second she saw the TIE zoom out behind her, Rey slammed on her reverse thrusters. The TIE fired its blasters, but its targeting was completely off. The enemy ship clipped the top of her cockpit and blew past her. There was no way the TIE could slow down now. It sped out of control, deeper into the narrowing cave. A few seconds later, Rey saw the glow of an explosion as the TIE ran into the cave wall.

"*YES!*" Rey whipped off her helmet and punched the air. . . .

But her excitement faded as soon as she looked around her.

It had just been a flight simulator, after all, but every time she took off the helmet, a part of her hoped she would have miraculously teleported to where she really belonged, back with her family—wherever that may be. She was still sitting inside the Imperial walker shell she called home. The sun still loomed large as it sank beneath the horizon. The blistering desert wind still scratched at her door.

It was an evening just like the countless others Rey had spent alone on the sandy planet of Jakku.

But Rey wasn't one to wallow. She shook off her disappointment and began preparing her pack for the next morning. There was a crashed Star Destroyer near the center of the starship graveyard she wanted to check out. Who knew what valuable salvage might be waiting inside?

Rey filled one last canteen and stuffed it into

her pack, next to her staff. If there were any dangers waiting for her, Rey would be ready. She had survived many battles, not just in the simulator.

But that was a worry for the next day.

The morning would come soon enough.

CHAPTER
I

DON'T LOOK DOWN.

Rey repeated that over and over to herself as she climbed down the side of the giant starship. There were more than fifty meters of rusty metal between her and the sandy desert floor below. Carefully, Rey reached down to a shallow overhang, looking around for a safe place to move her feet. The harsh wind of Jakku pulled at her clothes, but Rey held on tightly, slowly moving closer and closer to the solid ground.

With every move, Rey's prizes clanked inside her satchel. The spare parts she had found aboard the crashed ship would earn her at least one portion of food from Unkar Plutt, the salvage trader. Rey could stretch that to a few days' worth of meals.

That was how Rey spent every day on Jakku. She would wake up early each morning and grab her satchel filled with water and supplies for the day. Then she would mount her speeder and head out into the vast starship graveyard. Valuable spare parts were scattered across the desert plains—if one knew where to look. By the end of the day, she had usually found enough salvage to trade for a portion or two of food. If she was really lucky, she'd find some spare parts that she could use to repair her speeder or patch up the traps protecting her home.

On the best days, she would find old data chips that told stories about the galaxy outside Jakku. The dimly glowing words would conjure images of places Rey could only dream of. She would close her eyes and try to picture what the beautiful green forests or endless blue oceans on those distant planets looked like. But when she opened her eyes, she was still on Jakku. All she saw was the same desert that had stretched before her every day as far back as she remembered.

Rey's heavy boots thumped onto the burning sand when she finally reached the base of the ship. It was not the time for dreaming. She needed to carry her salvage back to Niima Outpost so she could trade it for supper and return home before sunset.

She adjusted her goggles and rewrapped one of the loose, dingy cloths she used to keep the fierce sun off her arms and legs. Then she set her bag full of salvage on top of her sandboard. Rey had discovered the smooth metal sled as part of a Mon Calamari escape pod a few seasons back. After liberating it from the pod, Rey could use the sled to quickly descend the largest sand dunes. It was practical—and a whole lot of fun.

Rey leaped onto the sandboard and rode it down the dune and toward her speeder. A smile threatened to reach her lips as the warm wind rushed past her. The sandboard didn't have the same smooth handling as her speeder, but that lack of control was also part of the thrill.

Soon the board skidded to a halt in front of Rey's speeder. She tied her salvage and the board to the speeder and zoomed toward the setting sun on the horizon.

As Niima Outpost slid into view, Rey could already see that the scattered tents and small spaceport were bustling with creatures of every shape and size. There was a long line of scavengers at the cleaning table. It had been a good day for many of them. Two Melittos hummed cheerfully as they cleaned off a massive panel from an old Trandoshan slave ship. The Melittos' sightless faces were turned skyward as they ran their supersensitive cilia across the panel. Even without eyes, the aliens could clean and repair technology as well as any sighted race. Almost all the panel's circuitry looked like it was in working order. Unkar would surely give them a week's worth of portions for such a find.

Rey hopped off her speeder and took a place near the excited Melittos at the cleaning table. The buzz of the marketplace pushed in around her as scavengers chatted about their finds, swapped tips about newly discovered wrecks, or shared news of explorers lost in the Sinking Fields.

Rey was eavesdropping on a particularly interesting conversation about a new Teedo settlement when she saw him. A little boy, no more than seven or eight cycles old, was exiting a nearby ship. Holding the little boy's hand was an older woman who, from the way she looked at the boy with such love and attention, must have been the boy's mother. The boy pointed excitedly at the strange aliens who passed by them. He must have had a million questions about the new planet. His mother reached down and playfully ran her hand through the boy's hair.

Absentmindedly, Rey mimicked the mother's loving gesture, softly stroking the salvage in her hand. Rey had no memory of her parents. She didn't know why they had taken her to Jakku, or why they had left her there. For all she knew, they were long dead. Yet Rey couldn't help hoping that one day a transport would arrive and her parents would walk down the ship's ramp and back into her life.

Rey looked down at the power cell she was washing. It had been clean for a good five minutes. Rey shook off her thoughts and carried her sparkling salvage over to Unkar's window.

The old Crolute's saggy skin wobbled as he pawed through the spare parts Rey presented. Why the blobfish-like brute had chosen to make his home on a dry desert planet, Rey would never know. Nor did she care to find out.

Rey tried to keep her conversations with the repulsive junk lord as brief as possible.

Leaning forward with a terrifying smile, Unkar made his offer. "Today you get . . . one quarter portion."

A protest immediately leaped to Rey's lips. *One quarter portion?* Her salvage was worth at least a full portion, if not more! But the thought of arguing with Unkar died almost immediately. Rey needed the food, and there was no one else to trade with at the small outpost. Unkar had seen to that personally.

Rey nodded and accepted the small packet of dried veg-meat and polystarch powder. It would have to do.

"Next!" Unkar called out as Rey walked back to her speeder.

That night, Rey took extra care as she cooked the veg-meat over the fire. She didn't want a shred of it to go to waste.

The smell of the sizzling food was

comfortingly familiar. Every night she took home the same veg-meat and polystarch rations. Technology was not the only thing that had survived in the starship graveyard. Most people on Jakku had grown used to eating the old Imperial rations for breakfast, lunch, and dinner. Rey didn't mind the repetitive meals; she just wished she could earn a fair portion. Rey's stomach growled as she poured the polystarch into a bowl, activating it with a splash of water. The powder quickly grew into a bread-like loaf. Dinner was ready.

Rey went outside, sat against the foot of the walker, and put on an old X-wing helmet. She had found the helmet ages before, and she liked the way it felt. Plus, the visor shielded her eyes from the glaring sun as she ate.

Rey tried to make the food last for as many minutes as possible, savoring each bite until there was nothing left.

Tomorrow, Rey reassured herself. She would

find something so valuable that even Unkar would have to give her a fair price.

Her simple dream was interrupted by a mechanical squeal. It sounded . . . scared? What kind of creature could make a noise like that?

Rey took off her helmet and heard the cry again, only this time it sounded softer and farther away. If Rey didn't act now . . .

She quickly grabbed her quarterstaff and ran toward the mysterious noise. It looked like she wouldn't be having a quiet evening at home after all.

CHAPTER
2

THE MECHANICAL SQUEALS were getting louder. Rey ran up one last dune and finally discovered the source of the noise.

Far below her was a Teedo riding a luggabeast. Rey took a second look around her and realized she was in the Teedo's territory. In reality, the small brutish scavenger had no more ownership of that stretch of desert than anyone else. But the Teedos insisted that they held sole claim to the lost technology scattered throughout the area.

And that day the Teedo had found quite a prize. He had trapped a little orange-and-white droid inside a rough net. From what Rey could see, the droid was not only in perfect working condition but struggling desperately to escape, beeping as loudly as he could. The dome and sphere that made up his head and body were spinning quickly in every direction. But what was a perfectly good droid doing way out there? And all alone?

There was only one way to find out. *"Tal'ama parqual!"* she shouted in the Teedo's native language.

The Teedo ignored her.

Rey was starting to get angry. The droid clearly did not want to go with the Teedo. Rey shouted again, this time making a veiled threat. *"Patqual! Zatana tappan-aboo!"*

The Teedo did not like that. He shouted back something quite insulting and adjusted his thick metal mask.

Rey barely noticed. She marched forward and drew her knife. As the Teedo continued to hurl empty threats at her, she cut the little droid free from the netting. Then she turned to the Teedo and said fiercely, *"Noma! Ano tamata, zatana."*

The Teedo did a quick calculation and decided the droid wasn't worth fighting Rey for. He raised a hand dismissively and turned his luggabeast toward the horizon.

Rey shot one more glare at the Teedo and then leaned down to inspect the droid for damage. Except for a bent antenna, the droid appeared unharmed, and he had plenty of fight in him. He rolled after the departing Teedo, beeping furiously.

To most people, the beeping would have sounded like mechanical gibberish. But Rey was good with technology and had studied the communication patterns of droids. And that droid was especially eloquent—particularly in his choice of insults toward the Teedo.

Rey couldn't help smiling at the droid's

indignation. "Shhhh," she breathed soothingly, placing a hand on his curved head.

The droid quieted down and then beeped inquiringly.

"That's just a Teedo. Wants you for parts," Rey explained.

The droid took that information in stride. He seemed used to being hunted down for one reason or another.

Rey knelt beside the mysterious droid. "Where'd you come from?"

He beeped an answer.

"Oh, classified? Really," Rey said incredulously. "Well, me too. Big secret."

If the droid wanted to keep to himself, Rey wasn't going to pry. In her experience, getting involved with others' problems only led to more trouble. She had saved the droid from being disassembled for spare parts. Her work there was done.

"Niima Outpost is that way," Rey said,

pointing toward the settlement. "Stay off Carbon Ridge. Keep away from the Sinking Fields up north—you'll drown in the sand."

When she finished her advice, Rey headed back up the dune toward home.

But she soon heard the whir of the droid's sphere moving across the sand behind her.

"Don't follow me," Rey said firmly. "You can't come with me."

The droid beeped again, pitifully.

"No!"

But the droid would not give up. He told her that he was alone and more than a little afraid. He had no one else.

That made Rey stop. She knew what it was like to be alone on Jakku with no one for protection or even company. Reluctantly, she gestured for the droid to follow her.

The droid beeped in happiness.

"In the morning, you go," Rey said firmly.

But the droid didn't seem to be listening.

He continued beeping, commenting on the landscape.

"Yes, there's a lot of sand here," Rey replied, only a little sarcastically.

The droid rewarded that response with his name: BB-8.

"'Beebee-Ate'?" Rey asked. "Okay, hello, Beebee-Ate. My name's Rey."

BB-8 began chirping again.

"Look, you're not going to talk all night, are you? Because that won't work."

BB-8 beeped the shortest response possible.

"Good," Rey said. She didn't know what to make of the strange droid and his "classified" mission. Still, it was nice to have some company for a change.

CHAPTER
3

THE NEXT MORNING, Rey helped BB-8 aboard her speeder and the pair flew off toward Niima Outpost. Along the way, she stopped to examine a few wrecks. She didn't want the extra trip to be a complete waste of time. If she found something to trade with Unkar, maybe she could even take the afternoon off and practice with her flight simulator.

To Rey's delight, she uncovered a pair of inverterlifts amid a tangle of crashed speeder bikes. BB-8 kept offering to help her look, but Rey didn't want to owe the droid anything. Even if BB-8 had helped, nothing else was salvageable from the speeders. Still, the inverterlifts would fetch a decent portion from Unkar. Her dinner plans secure, Rey raced toward Niima Outpost, with BB-8 beeping chattily behind her.

The brown and gray structures of Niima began to grow on the horizon, until the outpost's main archway loomed before them. Rey parked her speeder and set BB-8 gently on the ground.

"All right," Rey said. "This is where we say good-bye." She grabbed her satchel with the inverterlifts inside and slung it over her shoulder. "There's a trader in bay three who might be able to give you a lift . . . wherever you're going."

BB-8 simply stared up at her with his single black eye.

"So . . . good-bye." Rey began walking toward Unkar's stall.

BB-8 beeped and Rey started to laugh.

"Oh, really?" she asked. "Now you can't leave? I thought you had somewhere special to be."

BB-8 replied with a sheepish-sounding beep.

Rey had been teasing the little droid, but his response caught her completely off guard.

"You're waiting for someone. . . ." Rey glanced over at the spaceport. Every day, whether she admitted it to herself or not, she watched the ships come and go. She waited for someone— her parents, a friend, anyone—to arrive and tell her it was over. That she didn't have to wait anymore. That someone had finally returned for her.

BB-8's beeping interrupted her thoughts.

"*What?* No, I'm not crying!" Rey was furious at herself for her moment of weakness.

BB-8 made a noise that sounded too much like a chuckle.

"I was not!" Rey insisted.

BB-8 teased her all the way to Unkar's trading stall. By the time they reached his shady window, Rey was laughing at herself, too. She was still a little suspicious of the odd droid, but she was starting to like him.

Rey cleaned the inverterlifts and placed them proudly in front of Unkar.

"Two inverterlifts," Unkar mused. "A quarter portion for both."

Rey couldn't believe the nerve of the old alien. "Last week they were a half portion each! You said you were looking for—"

"Conditions have changed," Unkar interrupted.

Rey felt the anger rising. For too long she had allowed Unkar to cheat her out of the portions she deserved. She was about to say as much when Unkar surprised her with a question.

"But what about the droid?" he asked.

"What about him?"

Unkar stroked his fleshy chin with a smirk. "I'll pay for him."

BB-8 beeped furiously in protest. But Rey couldn't stop herself from asking: "How much?"

"Sixty portions."

Rey was stunned. That was more food than she had ever seen in her life. With all that food, she could stop living in uncertainty, worrying about scavenging enough parts for a decent meal. With that food saved up, she could start planning for a future.

She reached down and gently flipped a switch behind BB-8's head. The droid immediately powered down, his beeping silenced for the moment.

"One hundred portions," Rey said with more confidence than she felt.

That wiped the smirk off Unkar's face. He stared intently at Rey, but she defiantly held his gaze.

"One hundred portions it is."

Rey couldn't believe Unkar had agreed. It had been too easy.

As Unkar gathered the ration packets together, he couldn't resist adding, "Certain parties have been asking about a droid like that. I'd like to think this exchange'll be good for both of us."

He offered the packets to her. All she had

to do was reach out and take them and she wouldn't have to worry about food for a very, very long time.

Rey made the mistake of looking down at BB-8's still form. She could just imagine his indignant beeping, asking how she could even consider selling him to that disgusting trader. And the parties Unkar was hoping to trade BB-8 to were surely no good; they were friends with Unkar, after all.

Rey made the decision that would change her life forever. "Actually . . . the droid's not for sale."

She reached down and reactivated BB-8. As Rey had expected, the droid beeped out a series of angry accusations. Rey silenced him with a look and turned back to Unkar.

"Sweetheart, we already had a deal!" he raged.

She shrugged. "Conditions have changed."

"You can't afford to say no! Without me, you have nothing—you *are* nothing!"

"The droid," Rey repeated, "is not for sale." She glared fiercely at Unkar until he flinched and looked away. It felt good to finally stand up to the swindling trader.

She motioned to BB-8 and, together, the pair walked into the crowded streets of the market.

Unkar watched them go, his hooded eyes bulging in disbelief. Then he picked up a communicator and spoke into the rusted speaker.

"I have a job for you," he said, and slammed down the comm. Nobody spoke to Unkar Plutt like that without facing the consequences.

CHAPTER
4

REY'S STOMACH GROWLED quietly as she and BB-8 passed a food cart. The greasy steelpecker meat sizzled in the sunlight. She leaned down to the droid. "You're welcome for not selling you," she said pointedly.

But Unkar's words about "certain parties" interested in BB-8 were still running around her mind.

"I can't help you if you don't tell me who you're waiting for," she said.

BB-8 beeped at her questioningly.

"Can you *trust* me? *What do you think?*"

BB-8 couldn't argue with that. Rey had shown

him loyalty when he needed it most. Slowly, BB-8 told her about his master, Poe Dameron, and confided that they were on a mission for the Resistance.

Rey had heard rumors about the Resistance, but she had never dared to hope they were true. Standing up to the First Order seemed like a fool's errand. The shadowy military group had been created after the fall of the evil Empire. The leaders of the Order claimed to want peace and cooperation, but their brutal actions showed otherwise. World after world had fallen under their control, and yet the New Republic government had done nothing to stop them. Their quest for power was even starting to affect remote planets like Jakku. Just a few days before, First Order stormtroopers had destroyed a sacred village nearby.

Rey wanted to learn everything she could about the Resistance. She told BB-8 about the recent attack on Jakku.

BB-8 beeped sadly.

"You were there?" Rey asked in surprise. Clearly there was more to the little droid than she had thought.

Before she could ask him more about his mission, a stranger tapped her on the shoulder.

Rey turned to see a figure covered from head to toe in thick black fabric. Even his face was concealed by a pair of goggles and a rebreather.

"Plutt wants droid. We take droid. Female don't interfere."

"The droid is mine," Rey shot back. "I didn't sell him. Plutt knows that."

"You right," agreed the other thug. "Plutt knows that. You didn't sell. So he take."

His companion was already pulling a sack over BB-8.

Quickly, Rey pulled her staff from her satchel and prepared for a fight. The man in black held the bag with BB-8. He was her first priority. Rey swept her staff into his legs, forcing him flat on his back. As she lifted her staff to strike another blow, the second thug grabbed her from behind.

Around her, the Niima marketplace carried on as usual. Brawls were not uncommon there, and no one was going to risk making enemies to help a stranger. Rey was on her own.

Rey kicked the second thug in the shin. He cried out in pain, reflexively releasing Rey and grabbing his injured leg. The man in black swore and scrambled to his feet. Clearly, neither thug had expected her to fight back so well. When the man in black reached for the dagger hidden in his shoe, Rey yelled and ran her staff into his chest as forcefully as she could. The man hit the ground. Hard. One more thwack on the head and he was out cold.

Rey turned all her attention to the second thug. He was still cradling his leg, but he seemed to suddenly remember that he was holding a blaster. He started to lift the weapon, but Rey knocked it out of his hand before he could even blink. With one more blow, the second thug joined his friend, unconscious in the sand.

Rey leaned on her staff, catching her breath. Apparently, Unkar *really* wanted BB-8.

BB-8!

Rey ran to the bag where the droid was still trapped. "Hang on, hang on. I've got you."

A very disgruntled BB-8 emerged, swiveling his head back and forth. He was getting quite fed up with being captured. He spun his head to look around the market one more time and saw something that scared him much more than the Teedo or Unkar's thugs ever could.

"What's wrong?" Rey asked. BB-8 wasn't making any sense. He kept looking back toward the happabore watering troughs and beeping about a jacket. "What's so important about a jacket?"

BB-8 finally slowed down enough to explain. There was a man behind them, watching them intently. And somehow he was wearing Poe

Dameron's flight jacket. The man must have stolen the jacket from BB-8's master. Or perhaps even worse . . .

Rey was still keyed up from her fight with the thugs. Without thinking twice, she sprinted right toward the man wearing the brown leather jacket. She had time to watch his expression move from surprise to confusion to panic as he turned to run away.

But the man didn't get very far. He was clearly unfamiliar with the Niima marketplace, and Rey quickly overtook him. She slammed him to the ground with her staff, knocking the wind out of him.

She held her staff close to his face. "What's your hurry, thief?"

"What?" the man looked confused again. Rey wondered how he could have stolen something from a trained Resistance fighter; the man was certainly no criminal mastermind.

BB-8 rolled up beside them and extended a live electrical circuit. He pressed it against the man's body, shocking him from head to toe.

"Ow! Hey! *What?*" the man spluttered.

"The jacket!" Rey said, as if the man didn't know. "The droid says you stole it."

"Listen, I've had a pretty messed-up day, okay? So I'd appreciate it if you didn't accuse me of being a—*OW!*"

BB-8 zapped the man again.

"Stop it!"

Rey was running out of patience. "Where'd you get it? It belongs to his master."

Recognition slowly dawned on the man's face. He sighed heavily. "His master's dead."

Rey kept her staff pointed directly at the man's head. But any fight seemed to have gone out of him.

"His name was Poe Dameron, right?" he asked BB-8. "He was captured by the First Order. I helped him escape, but our ship crashed. Poe didn't make it." He sighed again. "I'm sorry."

BB-8 beeped sadly and rolled away to be on

his own. Rey almost wished the man were lying, but she could tell he meant every word. "So, you're with the Resistance?"

The man paused for a moment before answering. "Obviously. I'm with the Resistance, yes. I am." He glanced at her staff and repeated himself. "I'm with the Resistance."

Rey lowered her weapon and helped the man to his feet. She was still wary of him. Rey had paid dearly for trusting others in the past. But something about the stranger felt different. "I've never met a Resistance fighter before."

"Well, this is what we look like," he said. "Some of us. Others look different."

The man was clearly uncomfortable. Rey hoped she hadn't scared him too badly by chasing him through the market. Or slamming his head on the ground . . .

"Beebee-Ate says he's on a secret mission," Rey explained. "He needs to get back to your base."

"Yeah, apparently he's carrying a map that leads to Luke Skywalker, and everyone's insane about it."

Rey was stunned. "Luke Skywalker? I thought he was just a myth."

But any further explanations would have to wait. BB-8 raced back toward them, repeating one word over and over again: *stormtroopers*. The First Order was there.

CHAPTER
5

REY, BB-8, AND THE RESISTANCE

soldier peered around one of the marketplace tents and spotted two stormtroopers talking to some of Unkar's men. One of the thugs nodded obligingly and pointed right to where Rey and her friends were standing.

The man grabbed Rey's hand and started to run.

"What are you doing?" she asked.

"Beebee-Ate, come on!" was his only reply. But the laser bolts that ripped past them spoke eloquently on his behalf. They had to get out of there, and fast!

They zigzagged through a maze of tents as blast after blast followed them through the market. Finn was quick, but he had no idea where he was going.

"Let go of me!" Rey tried to pull her hand away.

"We gotta move!"

Rey wasn't trying to argue that point. "I know how to run without you holding my hand." The man tried to pull her toward Unkar's trading stall. "No, this way!" Rey took the lead, dragging the man behind her, with BB-8 close at their heels.

She pulled them inside an empty tent to hide. "They're shooting at both of us," she said, still trying to process how drastically her life had changed since that morning.

"Yeah, they saw you with me. You're marked," he said apologetically.

"Well, thanks for that!"

"Hey, I'm not the one who chased you down

with a stick," he replied. "Anyone sell *blasters* around here?"

Suddenly, they heard something outside the tent. The man grabbed Rey's hand and started running again.

"Stop taking my hand!" Rey grumbled. She could run from terrifying enemy soldiers on her own, thank you very much.

They made it only a few steps before a mechanical scream filled the air. A First Order TIE fighter whipped over them. The ship fired right into the crowded outpost, sending Rey flying. Flames engulfed the dry canvas, spreading quickly through the marketplace. Niima was in ruins.

Rey knew there was only one place left to go: the spaceport. She took the Resistance soldier's hand and ran faster than she had in her entire life.

"We can't outrun them," he said between gasps.

"We might in that quadjumper!" Rey replied. The beautiful ship looked like it had just rolled out of space dock. With the ship's powerful engine, they could easily leave the First Order in their dust.

"We need a pilot," the man said.

Rey smiled confidently. "We've got one!" All those hours practicing with her flight simulator were about to pay off.

"How about that ship?" the man pointed to an old YT series cargo ship. A giant tarp covered most of the spacecraft, but the parts that were showing weren't much to look at. Some of its paneling was loose, and the hull hadn't been cleaned in years. But it seemed like it could make orbit. Probably. "It's closer."

"That one's garbage," Rey scoffed. But no sooner had she spoken than a TIE fighter blew the beautiful quadjumper into dust.

Rey quickly reconsidered. "The garbage will do!" The trio ran aboard the old cargo ship.

There was one consolation in stealing that piece of junk: Rey knew it belonged to Unkar Plutt. She would enjoy imagining the fury on his blubbery face when this was all over.

Rey made her way to the cockpit and showed the man where the gunner's seat was.

"You ever fly this thing?" he asked.

Rey dodged the question. "Nobody's flown this ship in years."

She sat down in the pilot's chair and took a deep breath. "I can do this. I can do this," she said over and over to herself. It was just like the flight simulator at home. No need to be completely terrified.

Rey ran through the prelaunch sequence in record time and smiled as the engines roared to life. She eased forward on the throttle while pulling back on the control yoke. The ship blasted ahead in one smooth movement and took to the sky. Rey felt her smile grow even wider.

But her joy didn't last long. Two First Order TIE fighters were swooping down on them.

"Stay low and put up the shields—if they work," the Resistance soldier shouted up to her.

Rey strained to reach the shield modulator across the wide control panel. "Not easy without a copilot," Rey said through gritted teeth. No matter how much she stretched, the control was too far away. There was no way she could keep steering *and* turn on the shields.

For three insane seconds, Rey let go of the yoke and reached out to hit the shield modulator. The ship veered wildly to the right, throwing BB-8 momentarily into the ceiling of the ship.

Rey leaped back to the yoke and stabilized the wild weaving. "I'm going now!"

In Rey's hands, the ship banked upward and swooped down over the sands of Jakku. The TIE fighters were close behind, firing bolt after bolt at the cargo ship.

"You ever gonna fire back?" Rey shouted.

"Working on it!" the man shouted back.

After a few tense moments, Rey saw red bolts firing at the TIE fighters. Her new friend had done it!

"We need cover, quick!" The man called between blasts.

Rey scanned the horizon and saw the starship graveyard ahead. "We're about to get some!" Giant Star Destroyers and crashed starfighters were scattered everywhere. It was the perfect place to hide . . . as long as they didn't join the fleet of crashed ships themselves!

THE OLD CARGO SHIP sped between a rusting Mon Calamari frigate and a rebel A-wing fighter. No matter how close to the debris Rey flew, the two TIE fighters stuck right behind them.

Rey flew dangerously close to the surface of the desert, then banked hard to the left. The edge of the cargo ship cut deep into the sand and spun the ship forward. The Resistance soldier now had a perfect shot at one of the TIE fighters. He did not waste the opportunity.

BOOM! Pieces of the TIE flew everywhere as blaster bolts ripped through its hull.

Rey watched the remains of the ship fall to the graveyard below. All the TIE's primary systems would probably survive the crash. Some lucky scavenger would be eating well that night.

The remaining TIE stayed close on their tail. One of its blasts connected with the gunner's turret, jamming the controls.

"The cannon's stuck in forward position. I can't move it!" the man cried. "You've gotta lose him!"

Rey tried to shake the TIE by zigzagging close to jagged piles of debris, but it was no use. She needed a new plan.

In the distance, Rey spotted the hollowed-out hull of a crashed Star Destroyer. It gave her a crazy idea: if she could fly inside the ship, maybe she could lose the TIE for good. There was no way it could follow her into such a tight space. Right?

As Rey changed course to head toward the Star Destroyer, she heard the Resistance soldier's panicked voice over the comm. *"Are we really doing this?"* he shouted.

But Rey had made up her mind. She flew inside the Star Destroyer, then checked the ship's sensors. To her dismay, the TIE had followed them. Debris pelted both ships, but Rey focused on the opening at the other end of the Star Destroyer. If she could just make it through . . .

A feeling of peace overwhelmed Rey. She knew exactly what she had to do. "Get ready!" she shouted.

"For what?" the man shouted back.

Rey yanked the ship's yoke to the right and flew out of the Star Destroyer into the bright sunlight. Then she cut the engines, flipping the ship around so the gunner turret was pointed right at the TIE fighter.

The Resistance soldier took the hint. Rey saw the bright red bolts leave the blaster cannon and hit the TIE fighter right where it counted.

The enemy ship exploded in a hail of sparks.

But Rey wasn't going to wait around for more TIE fighters to show up. She flipped the cargo ship toward the brilliant blue sky of Jakku and set a course for space.

Beneath her, the sandy desert became smaller and smaller. The air grew thin and less turbulent. There were fewer and fewer clouds outside the cockpit window, and the first stars began to appear ahead.

It was over. Rey had outrun a platoon of stormtroopers, piloted a cargo ship for the very first time, and taken on two TIE fighters. Not bad.

She ran to the back of the ship to congratulate her new friend. At the same time, he was making his way forward to celebrate with her. They met in the middle in an explosion of words.

"Nice shooting!" she began.

"That was some flying! *How did you do that?*"

"I—I'm not sure. I've flown smaller ships, but I've never left the planet."

"No one trained you? That was amazing!"

"You got him in one blast! It was perfect!"

When the words ran out, they just kept smiling at each other.

Then a question occurred to Rey.

"What's your name?"

THE MAN'S NAME, it turned out, was Finn.
Rey figured he must have been on a Resistance
mission connected to the First Order's attack on
Jakku. But she didn't want to pry. His impressive
combat skills surely meant he was a top-ranking
soldier in the Resistance. Any further details
about his mission would probably be classified.

Instead of wondering about Finn's mission,
Rey got to work making repairs on the cargo
ship. Their escape from Jakku had damaged the
ship's motivator. Until Rey fixed it, they weren't
going anywhere.

Rey moved one of the grates from the floor
and jumped down to survey the damage.

"How bad is it?" Finn asked.

"If we want to live? Not good." Rey launched into a list of all the problems with that area of the ship alone, including a poisonous gas leak. She needed to fix the ship right away.

Rey immediately went to work stripping out the fried ventilation tubing. She'd have to borrow some replacement circuitry from the ship's secondary systems. Fortunately, she had a little experience scavenging spare parts.

After such an intense day, it was nice to get back to something so familiar. Once she fixed the gas leak, Rey tried to strike up a conversation with Finn. "So, where's your base?" she asked through the opening above her.

"Tell her, Beebee-Ate," Finn said. "Go ahead. It's okay."

BB-8 beeped obligingly.

"'The Ileenium system'?" Rey repeated. She was thrilled that Finn was ready to share some Resistance secrets with her.

Finn nodded. "Yeah, let's get there as fast as we can."

Rey did her best to comply. In no time, she had fixed the motivator and taken inventory of all the ship's systems. The vessel had certainly seen better days; almost every piece of equipment was in need of some repair. But at least nothing was on fire. Yet.

Rey made her way to the cockpit, where Finn and BB-8 were chatting. It was time to set a course for the Ileenium system!

But as Rey reached for the navigational controls, the ship shuddered around them. Then all the lights went out.

"It's the motivator, isn't it?" Finn asked.

Rey looked at the sensor readout. Her spirits sank.

"Worse."

"Worse than a motivator?"

"Someone's locked on to us," Rey explained. "All controls are overridden."

Finn ran to the window for visual confirmation.

"See anything?" Rey asked.

"Yes."

That was not the answer Rey had been hoping for.

"It's the First Order," Finn continued.

That *really* wasn't the answer Rey had been hoping for. Within moments they would be pulled inside the enemy ship and taken prisoner.

"What do we do?" she asked. "There must be something—"

"You said poisonous gas earlier?" Finn interrupted.

Rey was confused. "I fixed that."

"Can you unfix it?"

Rey stared at Finn. Then everything clicked into place. They could flood the ship with poisonous gas, taking out any First Order troops who tried to board. It wouldn't hold them for long, but it was better than doing nothing.

Rey and Finn grabbed a pair of gas masks from the ship's lounge and climbed beneath the floor grating. Then they lifted BB-8 down with them.

Finn pulled the grating panel over them while Rey worked on the console that would release the gas.

"This'll work on stormtroopers?" Rey asked as she pressed the release valve.

"Their masks filter out smoke, not toxins," Finn replied.

Rey was impressed. "You Resistance guys *really* know your stuff."

The ship's lights flickered back on. They must be inside the First Order ship.

"Here they come," Finn whispered.

Rey panicked. She still had two systems to reroute before she could flood the ship with gas. Time was running out.

She heard the cargo ship's main door open, followed by the clank of boots on the metal floor. By the sound of it, there was at least one soldier, but a softer thumping followed close behind him.

Rey worked frantically at her console. One system down. One to go.

"Hurry!" Finn whispered in her ear.

"I'm hurrying!"

"*Really* hurry!"

Rey was ready to punch Finn. "Does this look like I'm taking my—"

But Rey never finished that sentence. Someone ripped away the grate above them, exposing them completely.

They had nowhere to run.

CHAPTER
8

REY LIFTED HER HANDS above her head in surrender.

They were trapped.

But when Rey turned to face their captors, she didn't see any stormtroopers. Instead, she saw an old man with silvery hair and a blaster pistol. Beside him was a tall furry creature wearing nothing but a leather bandolier. Rey had seen only a few Wookiees pass through the Jakku spaceport, but she immediately recognized that creature as one of them. His keen blue eyes narrowed as he pointed his bowcaster at her.

"Where's your pilot?" the old man growled.

"I'm . . . the pilot," Rey tried and failed to say with confidence.

"You?"

The Wookiee howled a question to his companion. Rey had picked up a few basic phrases in Shyriiwook over the years on Jakku. That knowledge was finally coming in handy.

"No, it's true," Rey said. "We're the only ones on board."

"You can understand that thing?" Finn asked.

"And 'that thing' can understand you, so watch it," the old man said. "Get outta there."

As Rey pulled herself up onto the floor of the ship, she let herself feel some hope. The odd pair didn't seem interested in killing them. And the First Order would surely never employ a Wookiee.

"Where'd you find this ship?" the man asked.

"Niima Outpost," Rey said.

"Jakku? That junkyard?" the man snorted. "Who had it, Ducain?"

"I stole it from Unkar Plutt," Rey replied. "He stole it from the Irving Boys, who stole it from Ducain."

"Who stole it from *me*," the man finished. "You tell him Han Solo just stole back the *Millennium Falcon* for good!" He allowed himself to take a fond look around the ship. "Chewie . . . we're home."

Rey had to pause for a moment. "*This* is the *Millennium Falcon*? You're Han Solo?"

"I used to be," the man replied.

Rey's head was spinning. She had read data file after data file about that famous ship and its role in the war against the Empire. Thirty years before, it had fired the shot that took out the Death Star and ended the war. And that was just one of its many heroic adventures.

Finn looked a little starstruck. "Han Solo? The Rebellion general?"

"No, the smuggler!" Rey said, recalling the *Millennium Falcon*'s most infamous claim to fame. "This is the ship that made the Kessel Run in fourteen parsecs!"

"Twelve!" Han corrected. He was already wandering into the cockpit to check on his old chair.

Rey heard a cry of dismay. "Hey!" Han shouted. "Some moof-milker put a compressor on the ignition line!"

Everyone followed him into the cockpit.

"Unkar Plutt did," Rey said. "I thought it was a mistake, too. Puts too much stress on—"

"—the hyperdrive," Han finished with her. For a moment, he looked a little impressed. But then he said, "Chewie. Put them in a pod and send them to the nearest inhabited planet."

"Wait!" Rey said. "We need your help!"

"Help?" Han asked. "You've gotta be kidding me."

"Beebee-Ate has to get to the Resistance base as soon as possible," Rey said. "He's carrying a map to Luke Skywalker!"

That name stopped Han in his tracks.

"You *are* the Han Solo who fought with the Rebellion," Finn said. "You knew him."

Han turned slowly to face Finn. "Knew him? Yeah, I knew Luke."

Silence hung in the air until it was interrupted by a loud metallic *ka-chunk* from outside the *Falcon*.

"Don't tell me a rathtar's gotten loose. . . ." Han hurried out of the *Falcon* and into the larger freighter's cargo hold.

"Wait, a what?" Finn asked frantically as they ran behind Han. "You're not hauling *rathtars*."

"I'm hauling rathtars," Han deadpanned. He found a control panel and quickly flipped through image feeds from around the ship. One showed a transport ship docking with the freighter.

"It's the Guavian Death Gang. They must've tracked us from Nantoon," Han said, fear creeping into his voice. "I hate that."

Chewie roared questioningly.

"When someone who wants to kill us finds us," Han replied.

Everything was moving so quickly, and Rey still had one very important question: "What's a rathtar?"

"They're big and dangerous, and I've got three going to King Prana," Han said.

"*Three?*" Finn asked in disbelief. "How'd you get them on board?"

Han sighed. "Let's just say I used to have a bigger crew."

Chewie moaned in agreement.

Han opened a hatch in the floor and gestured to Rey and Finn. "Stay below deck until I say so. No bright ideas about taking the *Falcon.*"

"What about Beebee-Ate?" Rey asked.

"He'll stay with me," Han said. "When I get rid of the gang, you can have him back and be on your way."

"The rathtars . . . where are you keeping them?" Finn asked.

A terrifying *THWACK* from a nearby cargo container answered him. Rey tried not to take a step backward as a giant slimy tentacle slid menacingly against the container's window.

"Well, there's one," Han said.

"What are you gonna do?" Rey asked.

"What I always do," Han said. "Talk my way out of it."

Rey wasn't sure that was a great plan, but there was nothing she could do. She and Finn ducked through the open hatch and waited as Han, Chewie, and BB-8 went to confront the Guavians.

CHAPTER
9

REY TRIED TO BREATHE as quietly as possible, hiding beneath a ship's floor panels for the second time that day.

She heard the muffled voice of the Guavian Death Gang's apparent leader.

"Han Solo," he said. "You're a dead man."

"Bala-Tik," Han said in a charming voice. "What's the problem?" Han tried to convince the gang leader to let him go, but Bala-Tik didn't seem interested in that idea.

"Can you see them?" Rey asked Finn, trying to peek through a hole between two floor panels.

"No," he replied.

Rey crawled across the space to get a view of the Guavians. From her vantage point beneath their feet, it looked like there were at least six of them. The one she assumed was their leader, Bala-Tik, wore a high-collared leather coat and carried a huge percussive cannon. Behind him stood a handful of soldiers in red armor. Their faces were completely obscured by shining red masks. Rey could spot more than a few cybernetic augmentations that melded the soldiers to their armor and weapons. Han clearly knew how to pick intimidating enemies.

Bala-Tik demanded that Han pay back all the money he had borrowed. "Kanjiklub wants their investment back, too," he added.

"I never made a deal with Kanjiklub!" Han replied.

"Let's see if they agree with you."

Rey heard a portal open at the other end of the room. A group that could only be the

Kanjiklub Gang stepped into the already crowded cargo bay.

Rey heard Han address their leader. "Tasu Leech. Good to see you."

Curiosity got the better of Rey, and she crept back across the space to get a glimpse of the Kanjiklub Gang. There were only five of them, but they looked fearsome enough to take on enemies triple their number. They were heavily armed with different weapons, but they all wore identical expressions of fury as they glared at Han.

Tasu spat at Han in a language Rey couldn't identify. The meaning was clear enough.

"Guys, you're going to get what I promised," Han said. "Have I ever not delivered before?"

"Your game is old," Bala-Tik said, unconvinced. "There's no one in the galaxy left for you to swindle."

Rey heard BB-8 beep in fear. Things were not going well for Han Solo.

"That BB unit," Bala-Tik said thoughtfully. "I heard the First Order is looking for one just like it. And two fugitives."

At those words, Rey and Finn froze beneath the floor. Han had better talk his way out of that fast.

"First I've heard of it," Han said.

Below the grating Rey looked at Finn in panic. Quickly, she pushed herself back down the corridor, toward the hatch. But as she crept forward, the brace beneath her hand gave way. A loud CLANG echoed through the room above them.

It would be only a matter of time before the gangs started searching the freighter. Rey had to do something. Scanning the panels around her, she saw a junction box ahead. She crawled to the controls and began resetting the fuses.

"What are you doing?" Finn whispered.

"If we close the blast doors in that corridor, we can trap both gangs!" Rey whispered back.

Sparks shot from the fuse box, but Rey ignored their tingle on her skin. Just another second and . . .

One by one, the lights in the freighter died, until everyone was standing in darkness.

"I've got a bad feeling about this," Han muttered from the middle of his standoff.

Suddenly, all the lights blinked back on at once. As Rey reviewed her work, she realized she had made a mistake.

A big mistake.

"Oh, no. Wrong fuses."

In the cargo bay, three containers housing hungry rathtars opened.

"New plan!" Bala-Tik shouted. "Kill them and take the droid!"

A firefight erupted above Rey and Finn. They had to get back to the *Falcon* before they were discovered—or worse, eaten by a rathtar.

Rey pushed open the floor hatch and crept outside.

"The *Falcon's* this way," Finn said.

"You sure?" Rey asked, looking around for anything recognizable.

"No."

Rey followed Finn down a long corridor. Anything had to be better than waiting around to be eaten by a rathtar.

"What do they look like?" Rey asked.

"Horrible!" Finn replied.

They turned a corner and stumbled upon a scene of utter chaos. One of the gang members was tightly wrapped in the slimy tentacles of what could only be a rathtar.

The creature's flesh was covered in angry red scales that ran all the way from its round body to the tips of its eleven tentacles. On top of its—head?—were pulsing orange pustules that Rey guessed must be sensitive to movement or light; the rathtar had no eyes or any other apparent way of seeing the world. Most ferocious of all were the rows of razor-sharp teeth the beast exposed every time it howled.

"They look like that," Finn said as he pulled Rey away from the gruesome battle. But when they turned the next corner, another rathtar was waiting for them. Finn tried to run, but the beast had already grabbed his leg.

"*FINN!*" Rey shouted as the creature pulled him down the hallway.

Rey ran after the beast as fast as she was able, but she couldn't keep up. Soon the rathtar had disappeared, and Finn along with it.

CHAPTER
10

REY GAVE HERSELF EXACTLY TEN
seconds to panic. Finn was gone, and the ship
was crawling with thugs who wanted to capture
her and rathtars that wanted to eat her. But she
had to keep her cool. Finn needed her.

Rey scanned the hallway and spotted the
control panel that Han had used to access
holomonitors throughout the ship. She looked
through the monitors until she saw the rathtar
dragging Finn toward an open blast door—a
blast door that Rey could control from that
station!

Rey took a deep breath and prepared to time

her move perfectly. Just as the rathtar began to slither over the threshold, Rey dropped the heavy door right behind it. It was trapped on the other side, away from Finn!

Rey ran to help the traumatized Finn to his feet.

"It had me!" Finn said. "But there was a door!"

"That's lucky," Rey said with a smile. She guided him back to the *Falcon*, where Han, Chewie, and BB-8 were waiting for them. It looked like Chewie had hurt his arm in the fight, but otherwise everyone was in one piece.

"Move it!" Han shouted to them. As they reached the *Falcon*'s entry ramp, Han pointed at Rey. "You shut the hatch behind us." He turned to Finn. "You take care of Chewie."

Rey waited as Finn helped Chewie on board and to the lounge for treatment. Then, as soon as Han and BB-8 were inside, she slammed the control to raise the ramp.

Rey followed Han to the cockpit and sat next to him in the copilot's chair.

"Hey, what are you doing?" Han asked.

"Unkar installed a fuel pump, too," Rey said. "If you don't prime it, we're not going anywhere."

"I hate that guy," Han muttered. He flipped a few switches, and the *Falcon*'s engines hummed with power.

"Watch the thrust," Han instructed Rey. "We're gonna jump to lightspeed—"

"From inside the hangar?" Rey asked. "Is that even possible?"

Han shrugged. "I never ask that question until after I've done it."

BAM! A rathtar leaped onto the *Falcon*'s cockpit canopy, causing Rey to jump in her seat. Its rows of jagged teeth clinked against the glass as the creature tried to eat its way inside.

"This is *not* how I thought this day would go!" Han said. Rey couldn't agree more. "Angle the shields—"

"Got it!" Rey replied.

Han turned to the lightspeed controls and spoke softly to the ship. "Come on, baby, don't let me down."

He flipped the switch—

—and nothing happened.

"What?" Han cried, completely dumbfounded.

Rey calmly pressed one button. "Compressor," she explained.

Han flipped the switch for lightspeed again, and instantly the *Falcon* shot into hyperspace. The cargo ship disappeared behind them. They were safe at last.

In all the excitement, Rey had almost forgotten their mission for the Resistance. She still had to convince Han to take them to the Resistance base.

She decided to show him BB-8's map. Surely that would be the most compelling argument she could make.

They all gathered in the *Falcon*'s lounge and watched as BB-8 projected a vast star map above them.

Han studied the map quietly. Finally, he spoke. "Ever since Luke disappeared, people have been looking for him."

"Why did he leave?" Rey asked.

Han took a deep breath and explained as best he could. After the fall of the Empire, Luke was the last of the Jedi. He took it upon himself to teach the next generation the ways of the Force.

"One boy, an apprentice, turned against him. Destroyed it all."

Han was staring determinedly at the ground. He went on to say that Luke was overcome with guilt. So the last Jedi had walked away from everything and everyone. The Resistance might have been counting on Luke to save the galaxy from the First Order, but Han had his doubts. Either way, Han refused to return to the Resistance base.

But he did know someone else who might be able to help them. . . .

After a quick course correction, the *Falcon* zoomed out of hyperspace above a lush planet covered in lakes and trees. Rey stared out the window in disbelief.

"It's so . . . *green*," she breathed.

Rey felt very, very far from home. She had never seen a single tree before, and now she was hovering over forests that stretched to the horizon.

Suddenly, there was a break in the tree line and a beautiful stone castle came into view. Han set down the *Falcon* in a clearing nearby.

Rey walked down the exit ramp and took a deep breath. The air smelled . . . Rey didn't even have the words to describe it. But there was something clean and invigorating about the breeze that blew gently through the trees. It felt cool on her skin, completely free of sand motes and dry heat. The planet was both inviting and terrifying.

As they walked toward the castle, Rey tried to drink in every detail. That world would be a treasured memory after she returned to Jakku.

Finn gestured to the castle wall above them. "So, who lives here?"

"This is Maz's place," Han replied, checking to see that both she and Finn had blasters. "Maz is . . . a bit of an acquired taste. So let me do the talking." Han looked pointedly at Rey. "And whatever you do, don't stare."

"At what?"

"At anything," Han said.

Han threw open the big wooden door that marked the entrance to the castle.

As Rey stepped inside, she gasped in amazement. They had entered a grand hall packed to bursting with aliens and humans from every corner of the galaxy. Some were eating and drinking. Some were playing games of chance. All of them seemed to be having a good time. A band played enthusiastically in a corner with instruments Rey had never seen before. She didn't know if the musicians were any good, but they certainly seemed to enjoy playing.

"Haaaaaaan Solo!" a joyful cry cut through the noise of the grand hall. Immediately, everyone went silent and turned toward a short alien with golden skin. She was wearing simple clothes and a giant pair of goggles that magnified her eyes into big blue spheres. Lines marked every corner of her face; Rey could already tell the alien had earned them through centuries of hearty laughter and kind smiles.

Han raised a hand in greeting. "Hiya, Maz."

Maz waddled across the room to greet her new guests. "Can't be! My eyes must be malfunctioning," she said, shaking a finger at Han. "Last thing you said to me was 'Be right back.' That was, what, twenty-five years ago?"

"I've been busy," Han mumbled.

"Oh, trust me. I know." Maz shook her head. "I've lost count of the bounties out for you."

Suddenly, she turned to Rey. "Boy, are you hungry!"

Rey was stunned. "How did you know that?"

"Because your stomach's loud, and I'm short," she said, laughing. "Come—eat!"

REY TRIED TO MAINTAIN some of her dignity as a giant plate of baked cushnips with fral was placed before her. She waited for everyone else to be served and then dove into the food like she hadn't eaten all day. Which, to be fair, she hadn't.

Han leaned in close to Maz. "I need you to get this droid to Leia. It's about Luke."

"Then why don't you deliver it yourself?" Maz asked.

"I can't risk leading the First Order to the Resistance," Han replied.

Maz laughed. "Oh, yeah. *That's* what's stopping you."

"Leia doesn't want to see me," Han admitted.

Rey took a sip of the drink beside her and immediately gagged.

"Oh, yeah, don't drink that stuff," Han said, too late.

Maz smiled, then looked around the table at her guests. "I know why you all *think* you're here. But I feel there's something more. . . ."

She turned to Finn. "You. You say you're with the Resistance?"

"Yeah," Finn replied, a little too quickly.

"Hmmmmm," was all Maz said to that.

Then she turned to Rey. "And you? Who are you?"

Rey wasn't quite sure how to answer the question. She was seated at the same table with heroes from two wars. What *was* she doing there?

"I'm no one," she said finally. "Just a scavenger."

"Then you know machines!" Maz said.

Rey nodded. "Uh-huh."

Maz leaned forward. "Each component has a reason for being. A purpose. What is *your* purpose? Have you ever asked that question?"

Rey felt herself being drawn in by those big blue eyes.

"We all have a greater purpose," Maz continued. "Do you feel it?"

Rey felt something glowing inside of her. She *had* felt that but never understood why. How could a scavenger on a junkyard planet be a part of the story of the galaxy? And yet, in that moment, Rey felt certain that her destiny had finally found her. She opened her mouth to say "Yes!" when Finn interrupted.

"No."

Rey turned to him in surprise. "What?"

"I just want to get out of here," he said.

Maz pointed obligingly at a different table. "Big head, red helmet. They're bound for the Outer Rim and will trade work for transportation. Go."

Finn stood awkwardly and nodded to

everyone. "It's been nice knowing you. Really was."

Then he left.

Rey felt dazed. None of it made sense. Why would a Resistance soldier suddenly abandon his mission? They were so close to their goal.

Rey decided she wasn't going to let Finn leave without a better explanation. He owed her that much. BB-8 seemed to agree. The droid rolled close behind her.

Rey marched angrily up to Finn. "What are you *doing*?" Finn tried to turn away, but Rey refused to let him. "You heard what she said. You're part of this fight. We both are." She looked into his eyes. "You must feel something. . . ."

"I'm not who you think I am," Finn said finally. "I'm not special."

"Finn, what are you talking about? You're—"

"I'm a stormtrooper," Finn said.

That stopped Rey cold. It couldn't be true.

"That's all I've ever been," Finn continued.

"A stormtrooper has one purpose: to kill. But my first battle, I couldn't do it. So I ran. Right into you."

Rey's mind was racing to keep up.

"You asked me if I was Resistance and looked at me like no one ever had," Finn said. "But I'm not a hero. I've got nothing to fight for."

Rey quieted the voices fighting in her mind. If Finn really wanted to leave, there was nothing she could do to stop him. Maybe he was a coward after all.

"So you're running away?" she asked.

Finn sighed. "I think we both are."

Rey watched Finn make a deal with the aliens bound for the Outer Rim. Then he walked with them through the front door of the castle, without even looking back.

The merry buzz of the grand hall suddenly seemed distant. What were any of them doing there? What was *she* doing there?

Maybe she should just go home to Jakku and leave saving the galaxy to someone else.

CHAPTER
12

REY TRIED TO THINK of anything other than Finn, but his last words to her replayed over and over in her mind. To clear her head, Rey began wandering through the castle. The long corridors of stone seemed to stretch on forever. Rey made sure to keep track of each twist and turn so she wouldn't get lost.

Rey had thought escaping from the grand hall would help settle her thoughts. But being alone just intensified her fear. How had she gotten into that mess? What would happen if the First Order found her and BB-8? Were they still safe in the castle?

She found herself analyzing the hallways, marking good escape paths, noting areas that were especially exposed. From the moment she had left Jakku, Rey had been on the run from one enemy or another. She was tired of running.

Rey sat down and held her head in her hands. She closed her eyes and tried to focus on the happy sounds still echoing from the grand hall.

That was when she felt it—a tug, deep within her very core. Rey looked behind her and saw a stone staircase leading down into the castle. She had the overwhelming feeling that she was supposed to follow its lead.

She heard the soft whir of BB-8 rolling behind her. That good old droid must have been following her from the start. She didn't ask him to leave as she walked down the long stairway and into a cluttered basement room. Artifacts that must have been collected over centuries covered every open space around her. But in the center of the room was a plain wooden box.

Rey slowly walked toward it. It seemed to call to her, with a message she didn't quite understand. She gently touched the edge of the box.

Nothing happened. So Rey lifted the lid and reached for the strange silver object inside.

Instantly, a powerful mechanical breathing sound filled the room. Darkness pushed in around her until all she could see was inky blackness. Then a light flickered above her. She was in a dimly lit hallway covered with metal plating. It looked nothing like the stone passages of Maz's castle.

As she peered into the distance, she saw a man in black wielding a red lightsaber. His face was covered with a mask, molded to approximate a human face. But the mask's eyes were dead and empty.

The man's red lightsaber clashed against

a brilliant beam of blue. A young man with blond hair raised his own lightsaber and fought furiously against the monster in black.

Rey didn't understand what was happening. She turned from the battle and ran down the metal corridor. But as she ran, the floor twisted beneath her feet. She fell against the wall, which had somehow suddenly become the floor.

Rey wished that the visions would end. She was so confused. Where were they coming from? Why could she not escape from them? They felt so real.

Before she knew it, more images flashed through her mind: a hero stabbed by a fiery blade, a battlefield filled with soldiers, a blue-and-white droid beside a lost Jedi. She saw a man in a silver mask and dark hood, with six shadowy figures behind him. Without knowing how, Rey realized that he was Kylo Ren—warrior of the First Order. His red-gold lightsaber glowed in a frightful cross as he glided toward her.

Then Rey's vision shifted a final time.

She was back on Jakku.

Rey knew the landscape of that desert all too well.

But Rey was only a little girl in this vision.

She was struggling to free herself from a foreign hand that was holding her down like an anchor.

There was a ship.

Rey knew she had to get to the ship.

But the hand.

The hand held her back.

The ship flew away.

Rey's heart pounded louder and louder in her chest.

A figure emerged from the darkness.

Kylo Ren lifted his lightsaber and charged.

Rey felt a hand on her back. But this was not the same hand as before.

"There you are."

Rey spun around to see Maz smiling up at her. Rey was in the cluttered basement room once again. The wooden box sat innocently on the table beside them.

"What was that?" Rey demanded. She took a few shaky breaths and started to calm down. "I—I shouldn't have gone in here. I'm sorry."

"If you weren't meant to see what you did, the room would never have let you in," Maz said calmly.

Rey rubbed her head. "It must be the drink."

"It's not the drink. It's the Force," Maz said. "Frightening thing, the first time you let it in. But it's always present, at work in different forms— good and evil."

Rey didn't know what to say. It was too much. She was just a scavenger from Jakku, not a conduit for some mystical life force. She wasn't ready to be more. Not yet.

Tears threatened to fall from Rey's eyes. "Can you get me home?"

"Only you can do that," Maz said, taking her hand. "But ask yourself where that is. Return to Jakku to continue waiting?"

Rey nodded. "I have to go back."

"For someone who left you when you were smaller than I?"

"If they come and I'm not there—" Rey choked back a sob.

"They'll never find you?" Maz finished.

"Yes. Please . . ."

"They're not coming back," Maz said, not unkindly. "This I know."

Rey didn't know what to say. How could the little alien possibly know anything about her family?

"Child, the belonging you seek is not behind you. It is ahead."

Rey shook her head. "I've been away too long."

She turned to go, but Maz spoke softly behind her. "Quite the opposite."

CHAPTER
13

REY RAN THROUGH THE FOREST
outside of Maz's castle. It was too much. She was
tired of people she barely knew telling her how
she should feel. She just wanted to go home to
her simple life on Jakku. It was safe there.

Rey's thoughts were interrupted by a soft
beeping behind her. BB-8 was rolling along a
few meters away, carefully avoiding the twigs
and branches that littered the forest floor.

"What are you doing here?" Rey asked the
little droid.

BB-8 beeped comfortingly.

"No, you have to go back." Rey pointed at the

castle in the distance. "I'm leaving. I can't stay. I can't . . . do this."

She added softly, "Finn was right."

A beam of light crackled across the sky. Rey looked up, above the treetops, and stared in disbelief at the pulsing red beam. She could sense the power and destruction that emanated from the glowing light. Fear welled inside her. What was going on?

She turned to BB-8. "You *have* to go back. You're important. They'll help you more than I ever could."

The beam had disappeared from the sky. But in its place, a fleet of First Order ships descended through the clouds. Rey looked at the ships, then back at Maz's castle. Laser fire streaked through the air, blowing a gaping hole in the side of the stone building. Flames began spreading everywhere. Humans and aliens streamed from the castle, looking for safety.

Rey's friends were in danger. Even if she

doubted herself, she didn't doubt them. She had to go back and help.

Rey raced through the forest, scanning the fleeing crowd for signs of her friends. BB-8 was keeping up as best he could. Rey glanced back to make sure he wasn't falling behind.

That was when the shuttle caught her eye. Its enormous black wings folded skyward as the ship landed softly on the planet's grassy soil. An exit ramp extended, and a feeling of dread washed over Rey.

A man in a long black cloak walked out of the shuttle. Rey immediately recognized the silver mask that covered his face. It was Kylo Ren, the First Order's darkest warrior.

A platoon of stormtroopers accompanied him. Rey pulled out her blaster and ran for cover. "Follow me!" she called to BB-8.

But Kylo Ren had already spotted her. He was heading right for her hiding spot with his lightsaber at the ready.

Rey leaned down to BB-8. "Keep going. I'll fight them off."

BB-8 beeped encouragingly at Rey. He didn't want to leave her, but he had a mission to complete. He wheeled away beneath the trees and out of sight.

Rey kept her blaster drawn. Then she heard the menacing hum of Kylo Ren's lightsaber. It was now or never.

Rey leaped from her hiding place and fired two quick blasts at her attacker.

Kylo easily deflected both bolts. With a terrifying confidence, he walked toward her.

Rey fired shot after shot, but Kylo deflected every blast. Soon he was standing right before her.

"Tell me, girl," he said, "where is the droid I seek?" He lifted his left hand and reached toward Rey.

Suddenly, Rey felt a searing pain in her head. Kylo was penetrating her mind with the Force.

Rey tried to think of anything but BB-8. Her thoughts went immediately to Finn. Wherever he was, she hoped he was all right.

"You've met the traitor who served under me," Kylo said, reading her mind. "You've even begun to care for him."

The pain intensified as Kylo dug deeper. Rey tried to hold on tightly to every thought of BB-8, but Kylo ripped them from her grasp.

He drew back in surprise. "You've seen it . . . the map. It's in your mind right now." Kylo contacted his stormtroopers and ordered them to leave the planet. "Forget the droid: we have what we need."

Kylo flicked his wrist, and Rey felt herself losing consciousness.

When Rey woke up, she saw the weathered mask of Kylo Ren hovering above her. Reflexively, she reached for her blaster but then realized she was locked in an interrogation chair.

"Where am I?" Rey demanded.

Kylo paused for a moment before replying. "You're my guest."

He lifted a hand and the restraints around her arms clicked open. Rey tried to hide her surprise as she rubbed her sore wrists. She still wanted answers.

"Where are the others?"

"The traitors, murderers, and thieves you call your friends?" he asked. "You'll be relieved to hear that I have no idea."

Rey's relief was matched only by her anger at the cruel man. What kind of game was he playing?

Kylo clearly sensed her thoughts. "You still want to kill me."

"That happens when you're being hunted by a creature in a mask," Rey spat.

Kylo considered her a moment, then reached up and removed the mask.

Rey was stunned. She had expected the face

of a monster—twisted and scarred. But nothing about Kylo's face showed the darkness inside him. With his wavy black hair and dark eyes, he looked no different from the young men Rey saw scavenging on Jakku.

But when he spoke, Rey was immediately reminded of the power and evil concealed by his ordinary face. "I know you've seen the map. I can take whatever I want."

"Then you don't need me to tell you anything," Rey replied.

"True." Kylo Ren accepted her challenge.

He reached out with his mind and began searching Rey's thoughts for the map to Luke Skywalker. Again, Rey tried to clear her mind, but thoughts of her friends kept interrupting.

"You've been so lonely . . . so afraid to leave," he said. "At night, desperate to sleep, you'd imagine an ocean. I can see it. I can see the island."

Rey tried to pull away, but Kylo continued.

"And Han Solo. He feels like the father you never had."

"Get out of my head!" Rey shouted.

"Rey, you've seen the map. It's in there, and I'm going to take it," Kylo said.

"I'm not giving you anything."

Kylo reached toward her again. "We'll see."

This time Rey met his eyes. She pushed back against his probing thoughts, harder and harder, until the pain in her head suddenly disappeared. A flash of surprise crossed Kylo's face, and Rey pressed her advantage. She reached out with her mind, entering *his* thoughts.

"You . . . you're afraid that you will never be as powerful as Darth Vader!" Rey smiled in triumph.

Kylo Ren stepped backward, dropping his hand. He staggered toward the door, clearly rattled by Rey's power. He had just enough awareness to snap Rey's restraints back into place. Then he fled the room.

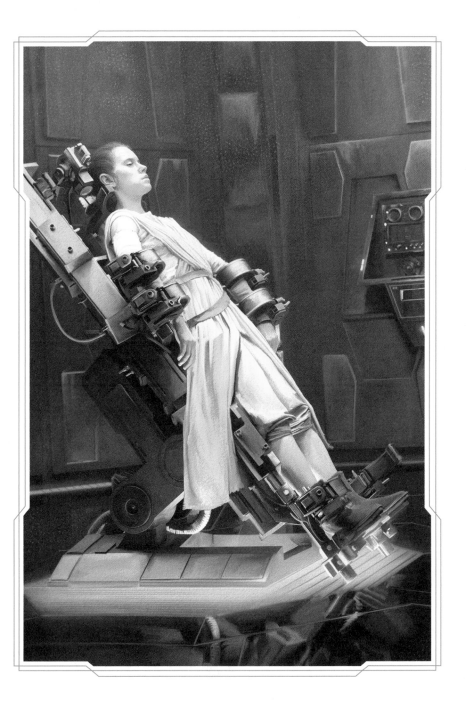

CHAPTER
14

REY'S MIND RACED as she looked around her prison cell. She was trapped, and yet she had never felt more powerful. Was that the Force Maz had spoken of? Maybe it was time she stopped making excuses and accepted the truth in front of her.

There was only one way to be sure. A stormtrooper guarded the entrance to her cell. Perhaps she could reach into his mind as she had with Kylo.

Rey cleared her throat. "You will remove these restraints. And leave this cell. With the door open."

That hadn't come out quite right. The

stormtrooper seemed to agree. "What did you say to me?"

Rey kept her eyes trained on the guard and let the power, or Force, or whatever flow through her.

"You will remove these restraints and leave this cell with the door open," she commanded.

Her heart pounded in her chest. It needed to work.

"I will remove these restraints and leave this cell with the door open," the stormtrooper repeated. He reached down and unlatched the manacles holding Rey down. Then he turned and headed toward the cell door.

"And you will drop you weapon," Rey added quickly.

The stormtrooper dropped his rifle on the ground, then left the cell. The door was wide open.

Rey picked up the weapon and ran into a gray corridor. She appeared to be inside a massive First Order stronghold. She couldn't feel the hum of engines through the floor panels. She must not be on a ship.

That was a setback. No ship meant no escape pods. A planet would be much harder to find a way off of. But which of the First Order's conquered planets had Kylo taken her to?

Rey followed the corridor until it turned into a walkway high above an empty atrium. On one side of the walkway was a steel wall, and on the other side was a straight drop-off to the atrium more than fifty meters below. The walkway ended in a giant hangar door and past that—a fleet of TIE fighters just waiting to be stolen!

The only problem was the platoon of stormtroopers guarding the door. There was no way she could fight all of them. Perhaps there was another entrance to the hangar bay back the way she had come. . . .

That was when she heard the clank of boots against metal. A group of stormtroopers was headed up the walkway behind her. She was trapped.

Rey glanced over the edge. If she climbed down, she could disappear before the stormtroopers spotted her. She tried to tell herself it would be just like climbing in the ship graveyard back home.

She ran to the edge of the walkway and spotted a perfect foothold.

Don't look down. Don't look down. Don't look down.

Rey slipped over the side and pressed against the stony wall. Above her the stormtroopers passed by without noticing a thing.

There were just forty-eight meters to go before she reached the atrium floor. As Rey looked for another foothold, she spotted an even better option. Just a stone's throw away on her left side was a service hatch. She could climb inside and use the maintenance tunnels to get outside of the First Order base.

Five tunnels, three hatches, and two wrong turns later, Rey felt sure she must be getting close to the edge of the base. The air was growing colder and her sweaty palms were beginning to stick to the cold metal floor beneath her. Rey saw an exit hatch in front of her and decided to take a chance.

She climbed into a—thankfully—empty corridor. Her blaster at the ready, Rey slowly crept toward what she hoped was the exit.

Suddenly, she heard a noise behind her. Rey pivoted, ready to fire, and saw—

"Finn!" Rey couldn't believe her eyes. "What are you *doing* here?"

"We came back for you," he said.

It was then that she noticed Han and Chewie standing guard behind Finn. Rey felt tears pricking at the corners of her eyes. After all those years, someone had finally returned for her. She didn't have to wait any longer.

Chewie moaned happily at Rey, and she smiled.

"What did he say?" Finn asked.

"That it was your idea," Rey replied. Finn had clearly embraced his role as a hero, and Rey couldn't have been prouder. She ran forward and hugged him tightly.

"Hug later," Han growled. "Escape now."

As they ran from the base, Finn explained what was going on. Kylo had taken her to a frozen planet that housed a weapon so powerful it could destroy an entire star system. The weapon was called the Starkiller, and the First Order had already used it to obliterate the New Republic capital. That was the beam of light Rey had seen in the sky above Maz's castle. Now the Resistance was all that stood against the evil group.

So the Resistance had launched a desperate mission to destroy the weapon. Finn had volunteered to be a part of the ground team, hoping to find Rey. He, Han, and Chewie had already succeeded in lowering the shield that protected the Starkiller. Now Poe Dameron—who was *not* dead, by the way—and his team of pilots were firing on the exposed weapon.

Rey and her friends finally reached the

planet's surface. There she was able to see everything herself. A squadron of X-wings circled above their heads, taking turns leading attack runs on the massive weapon. But Han looked worried. It was all taking too long. The X-wings should have been finished with their attack already.

They had to help destroy the Starkiller.

"My friend here has a bag full of explosives," Han said, gesturing to Chewie. "Let's put them to use."

"The oscillator is the only target, but there's no way to get inside," Finn said.

Oscillator? Rey knew that device was responsible for cooling powerful engines. The Resistance must have identified an oscillator within the Starkiller that kept the weapon from overheating.

"There is a way," Rey chimed in. "I've been inside these walls: the mechanics are the same as the Star Destroyers. Get me to a junction and I can get us in."

CHAPTER
15

REY PULLED THE LAST TWO WIRES out of place and reached deep inside the junction box.

They were right above the oscillator control room. Rey had managed to rewire the entrance hatch, and one last piece stood between them and their target.

"Been doing this all my life . . . never thought about it until now," Rey said, almost to herself.

"What?" Finn asked.

"One small piece can be so important." Rey yanked the control box from the base of the hatch and the door swung open.

Once inside, Han and Chewie divided the explosives between them while Rey and Finn stood guard.

"You take the upper levels. I'll go down," Han suggested to Chewie. "We'll meet back here."

Rey held her blaster high as Han and Chewie planted the explosives throughout the oscillator room. They were so close to finishing their mission. She and Finn even checked the upper catwalk and made sure the area was secure.

Rey looked down into the oscillator room below them, and her heart skipped a beat. How had she not sensed him? The evil pulsing around him was unmistakable. Kylo Ren was standing on another catwalk below them.

Rey held her breath and looked around frantically for Han and Chewie. She couldn't see the Wookiee anywhere, but Han was safely concealed behind a tall pillar. If he could make it to the hatch behind him, they could all slip away unnoticed.

But instead of moving to safety, Han stepped towards the catwalk and called out: "Ben."

Kylo Ren stopped and turned around. "Han Solo. I've been waiting for this day for a long time." He took a step forward. "The Supreme Leader is wise. He knows you for what you really are: Han Solo, small-time thief."

Han shrugged. "Well, he's got that part right."

Rey tried to process what was happening. How did Han know Kylo Ren? And who was the leader even Kylo seemed to fear?

"Snoke's using you for your power," Han continued. "When he gets what he wants, he'll crush you. You know it's true."

Kylo hesitated for a moment. "It's too late."

"No, it's not," Han said. "Leave here with me. Come home."

Home? Suddenly, Rey registered the resemblance between the father and son. But how? How could Han Solo's son have turned to the First Order?

"I know what I have to do, but I don't know if I have the strength to do it," Kylo said. The conflict in his voice was clear. "Will you help me?"

"Yes. Anything," Han said.

Kylo unholstered his lightsaber and slowly raised the hilt toward Han. He was close to his father. Rey saw the metal of the lightsaber flash in the dying sunlight. Han reached out to take the weapon.

But Kylo suddenly ignited the blade, and Han fell, lifeless, to the chasm below.

Rey screamed in horror. She couldn't believe her eyes. She stood frozen for three, six, ten seconds. Then a cascade of blasts snapped her out of her daze. Chewbacca fired a quarrel from his bowcaster into Kylo's side before setting off the explosives. They had to get out of there.

She took one more look down at Kylo Ren. Their eyes met, a flash of recognition crossing his face. He rose to his full height and headed for her with long strides.

Rey fumbled with her blaster, but Finn knew

the odds were against them. Stormtroopers where flooding the area to investigate the explosions. Finn grabbed Rey's arm and pulled her out of the oscillator room and up to the planet's surface.

Rey tried to focus on the ground beneath her feet. Somewhere behind her she heard the X-wings fire on the vulnerable oscillator. She barely registered its destruction.

Finn kept pulling them forward. Kylo Ren was surely close behind them. The red flash of his lightsaber caught Rey's eye.

Rey and Finn stopped for a moment and looked at each other. Silently, they agreed that they couldn't outrun him. They turned to face the First Order warrior. That was where they would make their stand. For Han.

Rey raised her blaster, but before she could even fire, Kylo used the Force to throw her backward. Rey's body slammed into a tree, knocking the wind out of her. Everything started to go dark as she fought to stay conscious.

She saw a beam of blue light appear and clash against the red glow of Kylo's lightsaber. Muted sounds from the battle fought to make their way through the haze that surrounded her.

Rey focused on the blue light, slowly rising to her feet. It was Finn! He was wielding a lightsaber. Rey raced over to help him.

Finn was fighting bravely, and Kylo was hurt from Chewbacca's earlier shot, but Finn was still no match for Kylo's practiced attacks. With a mighty blow, Kylo knocked Finn to the ground, wounding him.

Kylo used the Force to pull Finn's lightsaber from his grip. As the weapon flew through the air, Rey knew it would be her only chance to stop Kylo. She raised her hand and focused on drawing the lightsaber toward her. She felt a tug as it neared Kylo Ren.

But she was stronger. The hilt flew into her hand. Instantly, she knew it was the lightsaber from the box. She had seen all of this before.

Kylo. Kylo Ren was the apprentice whom Luke had trained. Kylo had fallen to the dark side. Kylo had sent Luke into hiding. It all centered on Kylo.

Kylo stared at the lightsaber in Rey's hand. "It *is* you," he breathed.

Rey didn't know what his words meant, but she was too furious to do anything but attack. She charged at Kylo and ignited the weapon. Instantly, the hum of the blade resonated within her. The lightsaber was unlike anything Rey had held in her life. She didn't understand it, but she inherently knew it was the most important weapon in the entire galaxy. As she swept the blue beam down toward Kylo, it moved as though it were an extension of her arm.

Instinctively, Kylo raised his lightsaber to block her. Their blades crackled as they connected. Rey took advantage of Kylo's surprise and put him on the defensive.

Suddenly, the ground began shaking beneath them. Rey realized that the destruction of the

Starkiller weapon must have started tearing the planet apart. A piece of the forest broke away from them and disappeared into a newly formed gulf.

"I don't want to kill you," Kylo said as their weapons sparked.

Rey laughed. "Don't you?"

"You need a teacher," Kylo explained. "I can show you the ways of the Force."

Rey wasn't buying a word of it. "You're a monster."

She intensified her attacks, sensing more than seeing where he would strike next. Her blade cut across Kylo's face before connecting with his saber hilt. Kylo's weapon went flying into the snow.

Rey stood above him with her lightsaber raised. He was defenseless. She could strike him down right then and end it all.

With a great rumble, the ground between them split apart. A deep ravine opened wider and wider, until Kylo was well beyond Rey's reach. Her revenge had been taken from her, but Rey had still won the fight.

She watched as Kylo stumbled away from the battlefield. His men soon found him and escorted him to an escape shuttle.

Rey returned to Finn's side and knelt beside him. He fluttered near unconsciousness. His wound was deep, and there was no way he would be able to walk. She wasn't sure how they would escape before the planet erupted into nothingness, but she knew it couldn't end like that.

She felt more alive than she ever had on Jakku. She had a destiny. It was big and frightening, but she had friends by her side to help her. Her life was only just beginning.

Rey held Finn tightly in her arms and waited for a miracle.

There was silence. Then the bright lights of a familiar spacecraft glowed above them. It was Chewbacca in the *Millennium Falcon*!

Finally, they were safe.

EPILOGUE

THE CELEBRATION STARTED as soon as they returned to the Resistance base.

Everywhere Rey looked she saw Resistance fighters happily reuniting. Each time it was exactly the same: the separated friends would see each other from across the room and race to be together. She watched the hugs, the tears, and the giddy laughter of survival repeat again and again.

Rey was truly happy for those brave soldiers who had risked everything to save the galaxy. And yet she felt a pang of sadness at every reunion. She mourned for Han and for the friendship they would never have. And she worried about Finn, who was still lying unconscious in the medbay. He hadn't woken up since the Starkiller battle. But the doctors assured her that they were doing all they could for him. All he needed was time.

Rey insisted on sitting at his bedside as often as possible. Once again, she found herself waiting for the return of someone she cared about.

It was on one of those late nights with Finn that Rey saw General Leia Organa. She was a powerful presence. The general had been fighting to protect the galaxy her entire life, long before she had become the leader of the Resistance. But now she looked tired and restrained. The previous few days had not been kind to her.

"How is he doing?" Leia asked kindly.

"No one seems to know," Rey said. "I guess treating lightsaber burns isn't something they cover in basic training."

Leia gave her half a smile, but it soon faded. "You have quite a journey ahead of you," she said.

It was true. They had the map to Luke Skywalker. Rey could go to him and learn the ways of the Force. She could become a Jedi and help heal the galaxy.

Her life would never be the same. She might never return to Jakku. She might never reunite with her parents. Finding BB-8, meeting Finn, running into Han and Chewie—a series of accidents had led her there. This time, she wanted to make the choice.

"If it were you in my place, would you go?" Rey asked.

Leia sat next to Rey and took her hand. "That's a decision only you can make." Leia paused for a moment, then continued. "But when you *do* decide to go—"

Rey began to protest, but Leia raised her hand. "Trust me, you will. And when you do go, promise me you'll be careful." She shook her head. "The Force is powerful. I know you must have sensed it when you fought Kylo. The temptation, the darkness can be . . ."

Rey didn't need her to finish. She knew that Kylo was Leia's son. The idea that the child of two such extraordinary people could fall to the dark side was frightening.

But Rey would not let fear of the past stop her from embracing the future. Leia was right: Rey had a journey to go on.

The next morning, Rey gazed at Finn in the medbay. She hated to leave his side when the future seemed so uncertain. But it was a choice she had to make.

She leaned over and kissed him on the cheek. "I'll come back for *you* next time," she promised.

Rey gathered her things and headed for the landing field. She didn't know when she would return, but somehow she knew she would see Finn again.

Chewbacca and R2-D2 had already prepped and boarded the *Millennium Falcon*. They were ready to take off. Leia was also waiting for Rey. It was Leia's mission to find Luke Skywalker that had put everything in motion. Now, with BB-8's map in hand, Rey was going to meet the lost Jedi.

Leia absentmindedly adjusted the collar of Rey's jacket.

"When I was young," she said, "I could have trained to become a Jedi myself."

Rey sensed Leia's concern. "As unprepared as I feel, I know this is right."

She had started to board the *Falcon* when she heard Leia behind her.

"Rey," Leia began, "may the Force be with you."

Those words were still echoing in Rey's head as she flew the *Falcon* high above Ahch-To. Rocky islands blanketed with beautiful green trees jutted from the water that covered the planet. Rey recognized the landscape from her dreams. She had imagined the place thousands of times without realizing it was waiting for her.

Rey landed the *Falcon* at the base of the tallest island. A rugged mountain path led from the landing pad to a small clearing near the island's summit.

Her destiny was waiting there. With each step, Rey felt it growing closer and closer, until she reached the end of the path. The clearing was filled with rough stone structures, and standing amid them was a man.

He wore a long brown robe with a hood that covered his eyes. When he saw Rey approaching, he pulled back the hood. Though many years had passed, Rey could still see in his eyes the young man who had battled Darth Vader.

She bowed and presented Luke Skywalker with his lightsaber.